Elijah's
Angel

A Story for Chanukah
and Christmas
by

MICHAEL J. ROSEN

Illustrated by

AMINAH BRENDA
LYNN ROBINSON

VOYAGER BOOKS

HARCOURT BRACE & COMPANY

San Diego   New York   London

Requests for permission to make copies of any part of the work should be mailed to:
Permissions Department, Harcourt Brace & Company, 6277 Sea Harbor Drive,
Orlando, Florida 32887-6777.

First Voyager Books edition 1997
Voyager Books is a registered trademark of Harcourt Brace & Company.

Library of Congress Cataloging-in-Publication Data
Rosen, Michael J., 1954–
Elijah's angel: a story for Chanukah and Christmas/by Michael J. Rosen; illustrated by
Aminah Brenda Lynn Robinson.—1st ed.
p.   cm.
"Voyager Books."
Summary: At Christmas-Hanukkah time, a Christian woodcarver gives a carved angel to a
young Jewish friend, who struggles with accepting the Christmas gift until he realizes that
friendship means the same thing in any religion.
ISBN 0-15-225394-7
ISBN 0-15-201558-2 pb
1. Pierce, Elijah—Juvenile fiction. [1. Pierce, Elijah—Fiction.   2. Woodcarvers—Fiction.
3. Afro-Americans—Fiction.   4. Christmas—Fiction.   5. Hanukkah—Fiction.]
I. Robinson, Aminah Brenda Lynn, ill.   II. Title.
PZ7.R71868El   1992
[Fic]—dc20   91-37552

F E D C B

Printed in Singapore

The paintings in this book were done in house paint on scrap rag.
The display type was set in York by Latent Lettering, New York, New York.
The text type was set in Cloister by Thompson Type, San Diego, California.
Color separations by Bright Arts, Ltd., Singapore
Printed and bound by Tien Wah Press, Singapore
This book was printed on Leykam recycled paper, which contains more than 20 percent
postconsumer waste and has a total recycled content of at least 50 percent.
Production supervision by Stanley Redfern and Jane Van Gelder
Designed by Lydia D'moch

Elijah Pierce (1892–1984) was a renowned woodcarver, lay minister, barber, and personal friend to many of his visitors. Elijah shared his work with his customers, fellow churchgoers, and neighborhood admirers for nearly half a century before participating in exhibits at such galleries as the Krannert Art Museum, the Phyllis Kind Gallery of New York, the National Museum of American Art, and the Renwick Gallery. In 1973 Elijah won first prize in the International Meeting of Naive Art in Zagreb, Yugoslavia. He was later awarded a National Endowment for the Arts National Heritage Fellowship as one of fifteen master traditional artists. What distinguished Elijah's art from the field of five hundred other woodcarvers was the personal vision that informs each of the works. The Columbus Museum of Art now owns the vast majority — more than three hundred pieces — of Elijah's work.

The author and illustrator extend special thanks for a Jefferson Center for Learning and the Arts grant.

ast year, when I was nine, Christmas Eve and the first night of Chanukah fell on the same day. And that day my friend Elijah gave me an angel.

Elijah is more than six feet tall and more than eighty years old. Elijah's angel is only one foot tall. Its wings are polka-dotted. Its eyes are diamonds. Its robe sparkles with glitter.

Elijah used to live in Mississippi, where his father was a slave. But now Elijah lives in Columbus, Ohio, where he has been a barber for fifty years. Elijah's angel used to be just a piece of wood until Elijah carved it in his barbershop.

I met Elijah when my fourth-grade class visited his shop.

Since the shop is close to where we live, I keep visiting. I walk there after Hebrew school on Mondays. Mostly I watch Elijah carve. Sometimes I whittle a scrap of wood myself, or I watch Elijah trim the thin hair of customers as old as he is. Some days I just walk around the barbershop.

The shop is one small room, as crowded with Elijah's carvings as Elijah's carving of Noah's ark is crowded with animals. Whenever I think that I've seen everything, the next week there is always something I don't remember. "Did you just carve this one, Elijah?" I ask.

"About twenty years ago," he replies. "That's pretty new."

Elijah's carvings hang on every single wall, one above another, up to the ceiling.
They line the windowsills, the shelves, and even the counter where his combs and
scissors rest. The curlicues of wood cover the floor along with the curls of hair from
the customers' heads. And Elijah's stories mingle with the hissing and shushing of an
old radiator, filling the shop with something as thick as singing.

A snake zigzags across a table. Crouched on a high shelf, a tiger bares its
toothpick teeth. Speckled dogs and teetering storks and lots of other creatures circle
Elijah's barber chair as if they were listening to his stories.

"Are the animals from the Bible, Elijah?" I asked one time.

"Everything's from the Bible, Michael."

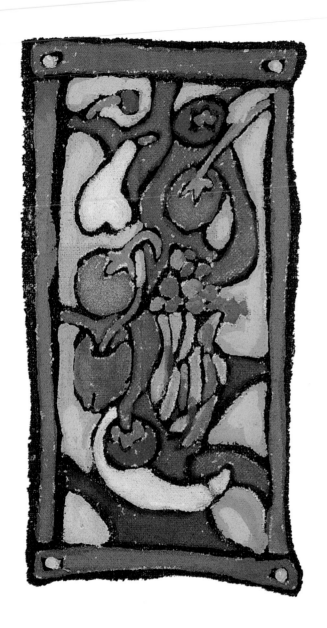

I am still saving so I can buy one of Elijah's animals — the pelican, maybe, or the dalmatian, or a new elephant whose tusks are made from a plastic fork.

We have one of Elijah's works in our kitchen. It's called "Fruits of the Earth": a tree bursting with apples, pineapples, pears, bananas, and honeydews. We're Jewish, so I knew my parents weren't going to buy Elijah's "God and the Angels" or "The Infant Jesus."

"Those are called 'graven images,' " my father explained to me. "Jews don't think God has one particular face, so we don't believe he can be pictured." I kind of understand that.

And I also knew my parents wouldn't buy Elijah's two-part picture "Slavery Days"; it makes them too sad — no, much worse than sad. I understand that reason a little better. In one half of "Slavery Days," black men are hiding in the secret rooms of a mansion on the Underground Railroad, while white people are upstairs eating a big dinner. In the second half, other white people are standing around a tall tree where black men hang from nooses.

My favorite of Elijah's pictures is "Noah's Ark."

"There are even two mosquitoes," Elijah always points out.

"The Book of Wood" is larger than the large table on which it rests. It tells about the life of Jesus, which I still don't know very well. But Elijah knows it by heart. If he doesn't have a customer, Elijah will stand at "The Book of Wood" and point to one of his carved pages and tell that part of the story. "The Book of Wood" is heavier than a cellar door. I have to help Elijah turn the pages. Elijah speaks softly, as if he figures I already know the story.

But I was telling you about Chanukah and Christmas Eve when Elijah was carving angels. All along the counter, a band of half-finished angels seemed to float around Elijah. I was counting out the diamond eyes for him when I asked, "Is there a story behind these angels?"

"Oh, lots of stories. Even stories about an angel named Michael. But I'll tell you about an angel I met when I was your age," Elijah said and walked over to his carving called "Obey God and Live." "Here I am in the kitchen, and you see the two books on the table?"

"Sure," I said, and I could see the carved boy that was Elijah and the carved lady that was his mother.

"Well, I reached right past the Bible and grabbed the Sears Roebuck catalog. That's this part, here." Elijah pointed. "So God sent down an angel and the angel struck me on the head. 'I told you to read the Bible, but you disobeyed me,' the angel said, 'so I'm just showing you my power.' " Elijah pointed to the hand that reached through the ceiling. "And here is my family carrying me to bed. They thought I was dead."

I've heard Elijah tell the story of "Obey God and Live" to lots of people. Each time, it's strange and eerie. He was my age when it happened!

Elijah returned to his chair and blew the wood dust from the angel he'd been carving. "So now just about everything I carve is a piece of the Bible. I should have been a preacher. People like to ask about my pictures, and I can tell them the gospel and they listen . . . like you, Michael."

Even though Elijah talks about Jesus and the Bible more than anyone I've ever met, I never thought about being the only visitor who wasn't a good Christian. I also didn't think about being seventy-five years younger or a different color from the other people at Elijah's. I just thought that Elijah and I were friends. We shared time together the way Chanukah and Christmas shared the same day that year.

"Here's another thing about angels, Michael. One is watching over you right now," Elijah said. "God created angels before he created people so the angels could guide us." I had heard of guardian angels before, though I was sure there couldn't be one for a Jewish boy like me. But I didn't say anything. I just listened to Elijah's hoarse voice and watched the flecks of wood flying from his blade.

We talked about school and whittled — I was making a whale — until it was time to leave. I wished Elijah a merry Christmas and we shook hands as usual. But then Elijah didn't let go of my fingers. With his free hand, he reached for one of the new, glittering, polka-dotted angels. "Merry Christmas, Michael. I want you to have this special angel," he said and placed the carving in my hand. "You know, I send prayers to all the wood I've ever carved; now you'll always be in my prayers."

I always pick up Elijah's carvings, but the new one felt strange: glittery and sticky from varnish — but stranger than just that. It was different from every other carving in the shop because Elijah had chosen it for me. I clutched the angel.

"Elijah, but . . . I can't," I stammered. "Someone may want to buy this one."

"Now don't go being polite. Merry Christmas," Elijah repeated. But how could I bring home a Christmas angel for Chanukah?

"Better zip it up inside your jacket," Elijah suggested. So I held the angel against my chest, and Elijah tugged the zipper up to my chin. I was afraid. Afraid of breaking it. Or smothering it. Or something.

"There," Elijah said. "Now you'll both keep warm."

I remembered to say thank you, but all I could think of was the angel pressing against me. What was I going to do? I did want the angel, because it was carved by my friend Elijah, but what would my parents say — a Christmas angel, a graven image, in a Jewish home? I thought of Elijah's carving "Obey God and Live." What if that hand crashed through the roof of our house? Would the hand seize the carved angel? Would it strike me on the head? Was I disobeying God?

I dashed through our back door, rushed to my bedroom, and sealed the angel inside an old tackle box I call my safe. Inside it are the silver dollars my grandfather gives me each Chanukah. But I could still feel the angel's eyes on me, watching me as if it really were my guardian angel. Elijah's prayers were coming through the metal box, through the closet door, through our whole house.

Before dinner, I moved the angel to my bookshelf. Then I hid it beside my bed so I could touch it as I fell asleep. I kept thinking of Elijah's "Slavery Days," as if the angel were hiding like a slave on the Underground Railroad.

The first night of Chanukah, which was also Christmas Eve, my mother and father and I stood around the menorah. I had made it out of painted spools and sequins in Hebrew school. It wasn't my neatest project, but my parents still put away their beautiful silver menorah and put two candles in mine.

"Will you say the blessing?" my father asked me.

My mother turned off the lights, struck a match, and lit the top candle.

"Blessed art Thou, Lord our . . . ," I said. In the glow of the light, I saw Elijah's carving "Fruits of the Earth." And instead of the words to the prayer, I heard Elijah's voice: *I send prayers to all the wood I've ever carved.* But then my father prompted me, and my mother lit the second candle with the first candle, and we finished the prayer together. "Blessed art Thou, Lord our God, King of the Universe, who commanded us to sanctify the Chanukah lights."

As soon as we finished I bolted from the room.

"What's so urgent?" my mother called.

When I returned in a minute with the angel behind my back, I said, "I . . . I . . ." and thrust the angel toward my parents.

"Oh, you shouldn't have, Michael!" my mother exclaimed. "Honey, you've already given us the menorah."

"But I didn't — "

"It's Elijah's, right?" my father guessed. "What a beautiful piece. Did you spend all — "

"I didn't — "

"Oh, good," my mother said, tugging me into her arms. "Thank you, thank you a million times."

"But you don't understand," I finally said. "Elijah gave the angel to *me*, for Christmas. It's a Christian guardian angel." Tears ran from my eyes.

"Don't be upset. We didn't mean to take it from you," my father said, wrapping his arms, too, around my shoulders. "Elijah's a wonderful man."

"But why didn't you show it to us sooner?" my mother asked.

"Because it's a guardian angel," I whispered. "One of those graven images we aren't allowed."

My father shook his head. "What this angel means to you doesn't have to be what it means to Elijah."

"It doesn't?"

My mother set Elijah's angel beside the menorah. "What I think it means is that Elijah cares about you. I think that's what he wants it to mean to you. It's an angel of friendship. And doesn't friendship mean the same thing in every religion?"

"I'm sure Elijah would agree with that," my father added as he ushered us to the dining room table.

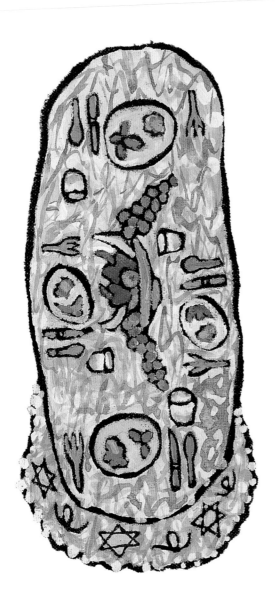

For dinner, we mainly ate latkes. I grated the potatoes, and my mother fried them up, just like pancakes. And then we called a lot long distance — to my mother's parents and my father's mother, to all my aunts and uncles and their families — to wish them happy Chanukah. I opened just one of my presents that night; inside were nine silver dollars from my grandfather, one for every year of my life.

When it was finally time for bed, I lifted the angel from the kitchen counter — the menorah's two candles were tiny wicks about to sputter out — and moved it to my nightstand as though it *were* about to guard me while I slept.

On Christmas morning, I peeled the hardened wax from the menorah and wrapped my present in Chanukah gift wrap. Then my parents and I wrapped ourselves up — in winter coats. Since there was no traffic, we walked down the middle of our snowy street, the only people outside. A Jewish family out for a walk on Christmas morning. We made it all the way to Elijah's barbershop without seeing a moving car or another person, and our footprints connected our house and his barbershop in a perfect dotted line.

A sign on Elijah's door read Closed, Merry Christmas. We knew he wouldn't be there. I opened the storm door and slid the menorah inside. Before I slipped my card under the ribbon, I read it to my parents: "Merry Christmas, Elijah. Your friend, Michael. P.S. Thank you for making me an angel."

My parents laughed, and my mother said, "*We* thought you already were an angel."

The next night, after we had lit the candles in our silver menorah, I asked, "Are you sure Elijah will like my present?"

"Let's go and see," my father said, and we walked to Elijah's shop. There we could see, in the steamy window, three candles burning in my menorah. The next night, and every night of Chanukah after that, before we lit our own candles, my father and mother and I walked past the crowded window of the barbershop. Every night another candle glowed in my menorah, standing among Elijah's crocodiles, tigers, snakes, and angels.

And even when there were cars driving and other people walking the snow-covered roads, our footsteps still left a dotted line between our house and Elijah's.